D0450303

Dear Parent:

Congratulations! Your child is taking the first steps on an exciting journey. The destination? Independent reading!

STEP INTO READING® will help your child get there. The program offers five steps to reading success. Each step includes fun stories and colorful art. There are also Step into Reading Sticker Books, Step into Reading Math Readers, Step into Reading Write-In Readers, Step into Reading Phonics Readers, and Step into Reading Phonics First Steps! Boxed Sets—a complete literacy program with something for every child.

Learning to Read, Step by Step!

Ready to Read   Preschool–Kindergarten
• big type and easy words • rhyme and rhythm • picture clues
For children who know the alphabet and are eager to begin reading.

Reading with Help   Preschool–Grade 1
• basic vocabulary • short sentences • simple stories
For children who recognize familiar words and sound out new words with help.

Reading on Your Own   Grades 1–3
• engaging characters • easy-to-follow plots • popular topics
For children who are ready to read on their own.

Reading Paragraphs   Grades 2–3
• challenging vocabulary • short paragraphs • exciting stories
For newly independent readers who read simple sentences with confidence.

Ready for Chapters   Grades 2–4
• chapters • longer paragraphs • full-color art
For children who want to take the plunge into chapter books but still like colorful pictures.

STEP INTO READING® is designed to give every child a successful reading experience. The grade levels are only guides. Children can progress through the steps at their own speed, developing confidence in their reading, no matter what their grade.

Remember, a lifetime love of reading starts with a single step!

For Lilly Grace—M.L.

Step into Reading, Random House, and the Random House colophon are registered trademarks of Random House, Inc.

Visit us on the Web!
www.stepintoreading.com
www.randomhouse.com/kids

Educators and librarians, for a variety of teaching tools, visit us at
www.randomhouse.com/teachers

Library of Congress Cataloging-in-Publication Data
Lagonegro, Melissa.
A cars christmas / by Melissa Lagonegro. — 1st ed.
p. cm.
ISBN 978-0-7364-2611-4 (trade) — ISBN 978-0-7364-8071-0 (lib. bdg.)
I. Cars (Motion picture) II. Title. PZ7.L14317Car 2009 [E]—dc22 2008047468

Printed in the United States of America   10 9 8 7 6 5 4 3 2 1

STEP INTO READING®

STEP 1

Disney · PIXAR

THE WORLD OF

Cars

A CARS CHRISTMAS

By Melissa Lagonegro

Illustrated by the Disney Storybook Artists

Inspired by the art and character designs created by Pixar

Random House 🏠 New York

It is Christmastime in Radiator Springs!

Oh, what fun
the holiday brings!

Lightning and Sally
trim the tire tree.

Mater hangs
lights carefully.

Flo serves oilcans
tied with bows.

Red has ribbons
on his fire hose.

Sarge leads
the group ahead.

Mater pulls
a big red sled.

11

Ramone paints stripes
on Lightning McQueen.

He picks the colors
red and green.

Lizzie sells stickers
to holiday buyers.

Luigi makes wreaths
from ribbons and tires.

Cars drive home
after shopping all day.

Sheriff makes sure they
are stopping on the way.

Lightning dashes
through the snow.

Mater is ready
if he needs a tow.

Guido shines
every snow tire.

Sally warms up

over a fire.

Doc fills Sarge
with antifreeze.

Mistletoe makes

Mater sneeze.

Fillmore fills cars
with nice warm fuel.

Lightning goes to snowplow school.

The town is filled
with holiday cheer.

Christmas is
the best time of year!